Snow Angels

A First-Start® Easy Reader

This easy reader contains only 56 different words, repeated often to help the young reader develop word recognition and interest in reading.

all
and
angels
are
around
back
be
bed
brother
bump
Bunny
by
come
did
fall
falls
find
flap
fun
everyone
go
hard
having
he
head
hiding
his
home
in
is
it's
lost
make
mother
my
our
out
playing
says
see
sled
snow
the
their
them
there
they
to
tracks
tree
we
where
white
wings
you
your

by Susan Hood

illustrated by Susan Calitri

SCHOLASTIC INC.

New York Toronto London Auckland Sydney
Mexico City New Delhi Hong Kong Buenos Aires

ISBN 0-439-68863-9

12 11 10 9 8 7 6 5 4 3 2 5 6 7 8 9/0

Printed in the U.S.A. 08

First Scholastic printing, November 2004

Where is Bunny?

Where did he go?

He is playing in the snow.

"Be my angels,"
says their mother.

“Go back out and find your brother.”

Find our brother? Where did he go?

Is he hiding
in the snow?

He is white
and hard to see.

Is he hiding
by the tree?

Is he hiding
by the sled?

Did he fall
and bump his head?

White snow falls.
It's hard to see.

Where is Bunny?
Where IS he?

Is he lost?

Where did he go?

We see tracks . . .

in the snow!

There they go!

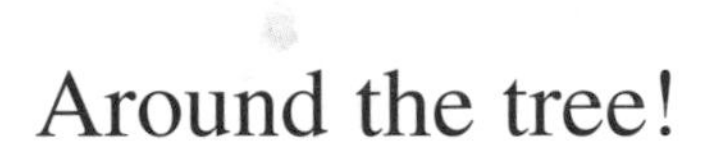

Around the tree!

Around the sled!

Come and see!

There is Bunny having fun!

In the snow, everyone!

They all make angels
in the snow.

They flap
their wings.
See them go!

“There you are!” their mother says.

"Come, my angels!
Come home to bed!"